RING

around

ROSE

by Sam L. Sullivan

To my wife Jan.
Next to Jesus, she's the best
friend this guy ever had.

ISBN-13: 978-0-9998226-0-9
ISBN-10: 0-9998226-0-8

Cover Design: Julie Sullivan
www.merakilifedesigns.com

TABLE OF CONTENTS

CHAPTER 1

FINEWEATHER

Saturday, June 5, 1971

Well, this is it, Rose Carlisle thought. I'm really here. Stuck for the whole entire summer at a place I don't want to be, with a grandmother I hardly know. Mom and Allen are gone. Just like that, gone. They barely stopped the car long enough to dump me out.

"This place is a prison," Rose had protested as they drove toward the old mansion called Fineweather that afternoon.

"It may be as large as a prison," her mother had said, "but the resemblance ends there. It's one of the loveliest old houses in this part of Arkansas. And you'll like your grandmother once you get to know her. She's even sweeter than her daughter."

Mother's attempt at humor was wasted on Rose.

"As soon as we find a house and I get settled in my new job, we can come after you if you like," Allen said. "Meanwhile, try to make the best of it, hmm?"

Now, alone in the room that was to be hers while she stayed a Fineweather, Rose only hoped she *could* make the best of it. As she sat on the four-poster bed looking at all the things she didn't want to take out of her suitcase, a knock came at the door. She quickly poked a finger under her glasses and chased away a tear she refused to let fall.

"Rose?" came her grandmother's voice. "Rose, may I come in?"

Rose jumped up and pretended to be unpacking. "Yes, Grandmother," she said. She wanted to add, *it's your house*, but didn't.

The small woman with smiling gray eyes and slightly graying auburn hair entered and went immediately to the window to open the shades. As

she passed, Rose caught the sweet scent of lilacs.
"There," Grandmother said. "It's much cheerier with the afternoon sun streaming in, don't you think?" She hurried over and perched on the edge of the high bed. "Are you finding everything all right, dear?"

"Yes. It will just take a while to get settled."

"Well, let me know if I can do anything to make you more comfortable." Grandmother's small hand swept around the room. "Do you like it?"

"Yes," Rose said truthfully. "Isn't this the same room I slept in when we visited at Christmas?"

"Um-hm."

"It sure is different. Before, it was so . . . so . . ."

"I believe *hideous* is the word you are looking for," Grandmother said with a laugh.

"It's almost twice as big as my room at home— or at least what *used* to be my room. Now, who knows what I'll have. Probably a tiny concrete cell in the basement."

Grandmother ignored her granddaughter's sarcastic remark. "I've redone the entire house since you were here at Christmas. I had just moved back then, you know. I had you in mind when I redid this room."

"Me?"

"You *are* my only granddaughter. I hoped you would come and visit me. I'm so sorry we haven't been closer all these years."

Rose didn't reply. She wasn't sure what kind of relationship existed between her mother and her grandmother, and she didn't want to be disloyal to her mother.

As if reading her thoughts, Grandmother continued. "I know things have been hard for you and your mother since your dad left. The truth is, I haven't been terribly easy on your mother the past few years. Hopefully, that's all behind us. Allen seems like a good man."

"Yeah, I guess. Mom seems happy."

"Well, that's *some* improvement."

"How did you know I like blue?" Rose said, bringing the conversation back to something less serious.

"Your mother told me. It's my favorite color, too. I had the walls painted powder blue, and I made this lace coverlet on the bed especially for you. I hoped you would love it as much as I do."

"I do. Thank you." Rose went to the window and looked past the big porch columns toward the wide expanse of mown lawn and the driveway that wound away from the house and disappeared down the hill. She climbed back up on the high bed and leaned against the ruffled pillows. "Grandmother, are you rich? I don't mean to be nosey, but this place—I mean, how do you . . . ?"

"Your grandfather left me well provided for, bless him, but Fineweather has been in my family a long time. My ancestors built it soon after they settled in Arkansas after the Civil War. Father and Mother left the land to my brother Ronald and me. I never expected to come back, so Ronald lived here. But he began to miss city life about a

5

year ago. He sold me his half for less than it would have brought on the market."

"How did it get the name—Fineweather?"

Grandmother made herself comfortable, as if talking about Fineweather was one of her favorite pastimes. "Well, the tradition, as my mother told it to me, is that her grandfather called it Fineweather because it seemed the weather was indeed more pleasant here than anywhere else he had lived. Believe that if you want to. In later years, I have decided that the weather *outside* always seemed fine because every generation that has lived *inside* has been happy. No matter what storm raged or what hardship befell the family, we always stuck together. This old house has truly weathered a lot of storms—both literally and figuratively." Grandmother gazed toward the window. "There are many fond memories for me here."

"Memories?"

"I grew up here. I thought you knew that. Your mother was born here a year after her father and I married. But surely she told you."

Rose shook her head.

"Your grandpa's job sent us away soon after Sarah was born."

"You seem too young to be my grandmother."

Grandmother smiled. "I'll take that as a compliment."

"You couldn't have been much older than I am when you got married." Rose swung down from the bed again.

"Five years older. I was eighteen. Back then, it wasn't uncommon for folks to marry younger—the girls anyway." Grandmother now spoke in a serious tone as Rose stood gazing across the lawn. "You don't have a young man hidden out there somewhere who is going to come and whisk you away as soon as my back is turned, do you?" Rose spun toward her grandmother, and the older woman's face broke into a wide grin that set her gray eyes to twinkling.

Rose was embarrassed. "No, I don't even have a boyfriend."

"That's just as well." Grandmother stood up to leave. "Tomorrow we'll drive into town for church. I wish I could promise you there will be other girls your age. You'd be welcome to invite them here. But the fact is, most of the young families have gone elsewhere."

"That's okay. I'm used to being by myself."

"Meanwhile, if you need anything, just let me know." Grandmother paused in the doorway. "You know, I think I'm going to enjoy having someone to talk to—woman to woman. These rooms seem awfully empty sometimes."

Rose appreciated being called a woman. "I think I'm going to like it, too. My mother and I hardly ever talk."

"That's a shame. She's a busy woman. Me, I've got all the time in the world." Grandmother left and closed the door.

With the scent of lilac perfume lingering in the air, Rose began to think that maybe the summer wasn't going to be so bad. She liked her grandmother more than she had expected to. And knowing that her mother lived at Fineweather even for a short time made it seem a bit more like home. What waited at summer's end hadn't changed, but she wouldn't have to face that for a while.

CHAPTER 2

MYSTERY GIRL

Sunday, June 6, 1971

Rose met several people at church the next day, but, being Rose, she said no more than "hello" when Grandmother introduced them.

After dinner in the big kitchen at Fineweather, Rose changed her clothes and set out up the hill behind the house. She was accustomed to spending time by herself at home and at school, but with so much territory to explore and no one to share it with, she couldn't help feeling alone.

The sun shone brightly, but the breeze only hinted of the dog days to come. The ground was soft and damp from recent rain, and the woods smelled of pine and rotting wood. A small creek trickled past a grassy slope. Rose picked a yellow wildflower, sniffed it, and tossed it into the water. When it disappeared into the distance, she picked another. She sat on a large rock on the bank, where she could see several yards up the creek. After a while, she thought she saw something move just on the other side of a thick bush. She went a little closer and peered from behind an overhanging tree.

There was a girl in a white dress sitting on another rock, looking upstream with her back to Rose. When the girl looked in her direction, Rose ducked behind the tree. She wanted to speak. She even opened her mouth once, but nothing came out. She started to leave and then turned for another look. The girl had moved farther up the creek and was walking away quickly. Rose followed for a while and then decided she should head back. Suddenly she became aware of how far she had walked. At first, she feared she was lost, but then she realized she need only follow the creek back to where she had begun.

"DID YOU have a nice excursion today, shug?" Grandmother said that evening at supper.

"Oh, yes," Rose said. "Everything is pretty—so quiet and peaceful. Not like I'm used to."

"I know. It's one of the reasons I came back here."

"I walked down to that creek on the other side of the pine grove."

"Sand Creek. I've been there many a time in my younger years."

"Grandmother, does anyone else live around here?"

"My cousin Bill lives a few miles down the road."

"Does he have a daughter?"

Grandmother nodded. "Betty is married and lives in Tennessee."

"I saw a girl down by the creek."

Grandmother's brow wrinkled and she looked very serious for a moment. "What sort of girl?"

"About my age and size, and she had red hair like mine. I didn't get a good look at her face, but I was certain she was one of my long-lost relatives."

Grandmother's eyes brightened and her face took on the look a face sometimes wears when it hides a secret. "Did you speak to her?"

Rose shook her head. "I wanted to. She didn't seem to notice me. What is it, grandmother? Why are you smiling at me like that?"

Grandmother didn't answer. She got up and began to clear away the dishes. "Did you go any farther than the creek?"

"Not much."

"Do be careful out there, dear. Long ago, I knew this whole estate like the back of my hand. Now, I'm not sure I could find you if you became lost."

"Don't worry, I can find my way around." Rose went to the sink and began to rinse the dishes and stack them out to dry. "Grandmother, where do you suppose that girl lives? She must have been a long way from home."

Grandmother finally broke her thoughtful silence. She stopped scrubbing plates and looked squarely at Rose. "I'm not certain I want to tell you this, and it might not have anything to do with the girl you saw. It's about the Peabody Place."

"Where's that?"

"Just across the meadow from the creek. If you had gone much farther, you would have seen it."

"That's where the girl lives?"

"I wouldn't think so. The place must be terribly run down, and it never was much more than a shack. Families lived there who worked for my father and grandfather. I suppose some of them were named Peabody. I don't recall anyone living there since I was a teenager. Anyone who lived there now would have to be awfully destitute. Besides which, they would be on *my* property."

"You said you weren't sure you wanted to tell me about it. Does that mean I am forbidden to go there?"

"No, I see no reason for that. I'm satisfied no one lives there. I just want to warn you to be extra careful."

"I will." Rose placed the last dish onto the drainer, dried her hands, and hung the towel on the rod. She knew exactly where her exploring tomorrow would take her.

CHAPTER 3

THE PEABODY PLACE

Monday, June 7, 1971

Weeds and bushes covered the yard and all but engulfed the foundation of the old house. A wild morning glory vine had found a crack between two boards on the porch and wound its way up one of the posts. The roof of the porch was sagging on one side, but the floorboards supported Rose's weight, creaking and groaning. She swung open the rough gray door and peered in.

Except for a ragged brown sofa in the middle of the floor and a dusty metal trunk next to the fireplace, the shack was empty. Remembering Grandmother's warning, Rose moved slowly, carefully studying each spot on the floor where her foot would fall next. Then, satisfied that the floor was strong, she walked less cautiously.

The air was still and warm. Rose tried to open some windows, but most were hopelessly sealed by time and weather. As she managed to lift one, a big red wasp buzzed in from the porch. It made a few circles around her head and then disappeared back out the window.

The shack had three rooms. The two smallest ones were totally bare. Long-cold ashes covered the bottom of the fireplace in the big room, and cobwebs sagged under the weight of years of collected dust.

Rose started to sit on the trunk and decided to open it instead. She dragged it by one of its rusted handles until it sat beneath the open front window. She blew dust from the latch and quickly fanned her hand in front of her face. Gently, she lifted the bent lid and let it fall back against the windowsill.

Papers—that seemed to be all there was in the trunk. She dug through them, glancing at one now and then. At the bottom, a tiny pink plastic foot protruded from beneath a parched envelope.

She freed the rest of the doll and examined it. The head was totally made of plastic and had painted brown hair and painted blue eyes, not like any doll Rose had ever seen. The faded green dress was poorly sewn, as if made by a child. Rose scratched beneath the last of the papers and then shut the trunk.

She carried the doll out onto the porch. Nearby, a squirrel flicked its tail and disappeared up a tree. Birds sang in the woods, and a crow cried *"caw-caw"* high above. The late afternoon sun was falling behind the trees. Rose knew she would have to start home soon if she was to make it before dark.

Whose doll is this? she wondered. Why was it left here? Maybe Grandmother would have a clue. She started for Fineweather, and then, thinking she heard a voice behind her, she turned to look back. The girl in the white dress stood at the front window of the shack.

"She's here!" Rose whispered. She was in the shadows by now, and she ducked behind a big tree and peeked out. Had she been seen?

The girl in the white dress disappeared from the window for a moment, as if stooping to take something from the trunk. Then she raised up and looked out again. The doll must be hers, Rose thought. She's looking for it in the trunk.

Rose kept her eyes on the figure in the window and inched from behind the tree. She eased into the fading sunlight and stopped. The girl inside continued to stare silently. Rose raised her hand to wave and call to the girl, but instead, she dropped her hand quickly and started toward home. When she glanced back once more, the girl was gone from the window.

GRANDMOTHER HAD supper prepared when Rose flew through the screen door into the kitchen. "Goodness, dear," she said, "you look as if you've run ten miles."

"I think I did," Rose said breathlessly.

"I thought I was going to have to leave you a note," Grandmother said, removing her apron. "I've already eaten. You'll have to serve yourself. Meda Hutton called. She desperately needs help with a church project that should have been finished last week, to hear her tell it. You'd be welcome to come along, but you haven't eaten, and I must leave right away."

Rose shook her head then caught her glasses, which were about to slip off the end of her moist nose. "That's okay. But Grandmother, let me tell you—"

"Sorry, shug," came Grandmother's voice from the hallway. "I know I said I always have time on my hands, but—well, if you knew Meda Hutton, you'd understand. I'll be gone a couple of hours."

Rose had finished a lonely supper, showered, and was preparing for bed when Grandmother breezed into her room, bringing the scent of flowers.

Rose finished brushing her hair. "I thought you said a couple of hours."

"Yes, I did." Grandmother took a seat on the corner of the bed and daubed her face with a lace handkerchief. "Every time I go over there, I tell myself I won't stay long. But that woman!"

Rose hopped on the bed and leaned against the high wooden headboard. Grandmother stood up and straightened the bedsheet and then sat down again. "So, what happened today that excited you so that you ran all the back to tell me?"

"You said I could visit the Peabody Place, right?"

Grandmother smiled. "Actually, I believe I just didn't forbid it. I knew keeping you away from there would be as easy as getting away from Sister Hutton."

"Grandmother . . ." Rose squinted at her grandmother and then held up her hand to put a hold on the conversation while she fetched her glasses from the bedside table. "Grandmother, are there ghosts here?"

"*Ghosts* now, is it?" Grandmother crossed her arms and leaned against a post at the foot of the bed. Rose thought about how differently her mother would have reacted. Mother would have made some sort of harrumphing noise and disappeared from the room. "Lands, I hope there aren't any ghosts. Did you see one?"

"I saw that girl again." Rose pulled the tattered doll out of the drawer in the bedside table. "And I found this."

"Well, I'll say!" Grandmother took the doll and turned it over in her hands to examine it closely. "They sure don't make them like this anymore. No telling how old it is."

"I think it's hers. It was in an old trunk I found in the shack."

"You went in?"

"I was careful."

"And where was the girl?"

"That's the strange part. I looked in every room of the shack, and there was no one there. I'm sure there wasn't. But when I started to leave, there she was—at the window. Does that place have a back door?"

"I don't recall. I haven't been out there in ages. A window maybe?"

"The windows were all stuck except one, and I could see it the whole time."

"Did it look as if someone has been in there?"

"No, everything was dirty. There was no furniture except an old couch."

"So did you speak to the girl this time?"

"I wanted to, but I couldn't. She didn't speak to me either. There you go looking at me like that again. What is it, Grandmother?"

"This is becoming so interesting. I would love to know more about your mystery girl. Wouldn't you?"

"I sure would. If only she would say something."

"Maybe it's up to *you* to make the first move." Grandmother stood up to leave.

"Oh, Grandmother, you don't mind her being on your land, do you?"

"Umm, I think not. She sounds harmless enough." Grandmother was near the door, and she returned suddenly to Rose's bedside. "I almost forgot to tell you some news I heard tonight. You know I told you that our nearest neighbors live a few miles from here."

"Um-hm."

"Well, apparently, we have a new neighbor. Sister Hutton said a piece of property next to mine was sold last week. A man named Dooley Birdsong has moved into a little shanty just east of us."

"Maybe he has a daughter."

"As far as we know, it's just him. No one knows much about him. No one's seen him except Mr. Everett down at the store. I just want to remind you . . . ."

"I know, be careful."

"That's right." Grandmother flipped out the light. As her steps faded down the hallway, Rose lay in bed thinking. If the doll did belong to the mystery girl, then she must have lived at the

Peabody Place when she was little. Rose had to find out. And she would do it tomorrow.

CHAPTER 4

HIDDEN TREASURE

Tuesday, June 8, 1971

"Oh, no! It's raining!" Rose moaned when she looked out the window the next morning. Sheets of water were cascading off the high roof and splashing to the ground below.

"Well, it won't rain forever," Grandmother said when Rose went downstairs. "You know what they say about Arkansas weather. If you don't like it, stick around—it will soon change."

"But now that girl will probably go away and I'll never see her again. Or I might lose my nerve. That's the way it always happens."

"I don't think you need to give up so soon. Meanwhile, after breakfast, why don't I show you the rest of the house? This place has rooms even *I* don't see for weeks at a time."

THE TOUR took almost an hour. Many of Fineweather's rooms were empty, but Grandmother recounted interesting histories of some of them and shared her own memories with Rose. The last stop was the attic, which Rose discovered by accident.

At the end of the second-floor hallway was a narrow door, which Rose had assumed was a closet. But when she peeked inside, she discovered a steep stairway that beckoned toward the rafters. She was already at the top of the stairs when Grandmother discovered her missing and followed.

There was room to stand up. On three of the four sides were double windows that let in plenty of light. Facing toward the rear of the house was a dormer, over which the roof jutted out enough so that the window could be opened without letting in the rain.

"What a mess!" Grandmother said. "I keep telling myself I'll get up here and sort through some of this stuff, but mercy . . . ."

"I love it!" Rose said as she scratched through stacks of books, old vinyl records, clothing, broken furniture, toys, and discarded flower pots. "Is all this stuff yours?"

Grandmother heaved a sigh. "I suppose it is now, though most of it has been here much longer than I have."

Rose was most interested in a trunk which sat half hidden in a corner. It was larger than the one she had found at the Peabody Place and in better condition. She pushed the catch and tugged at the lid. It didn't budge. She pounded the latch with her fist. "It's stuck!"

"Locked," Grandmother said.

"Where's the key?"

"Hon, your guess is as good as mine." Grandmother and Rose scratched around the trunk, to no avail. "I suppose the key could be stashed away downstairs—if it exists at all."

"Let's find it," Rose said eagerly. "Right now. Maybe there's a treasure hidden in there."

"I doubt that. My ancestors knew how to invest their money. Still, I'm a little curious myself." Grandmother dusted her hands together. "But it's awfully warm up here, don't you think? Perhaps we'll come back later this evening or in the morning."

Rose didn't answer as she shot down the steep stairs. The first place she looked was in the drawer of a tiny round table that sat just outside the door to the attic. Then she and Grandmother looked in all the other logical places: bedside tables, bureaus, kitchen cupboards, the bookshelves in the living room.

"Maybe there is a secret hiding place," said Rose.

"Maybe the key's just lost," Grandmother said, plopping herself on the large chair beside the hearth, "in which case, it would take a locksmith to open the trunk."

"No! It can't be." Rose sat in the middle of the room searching for ideas. Her eyes fell on the mantle. "In movies, they hide things behind loose bricks in the fireplace."

"There are no loose bricks in that fireplace."

Rose ran her hand over every brick she could reach. Then she stood on tiptoe and looked above the high mantel. "What about the brick wall behind the stove in the kitchen?"

Grandmother shook her head. "Those are fake. I had them put there myself."

"Then where can it be?" Rose said in desperation. She went back to the bookshelf beside the fireplace. She was about to remove a large book from the shelf when something caught her eye. There was a narrow crack where the heavy wooden mantle joined the brick on one side, and in that crack was something shiny. She carefully pushed the object out with a letter opener which lay on the mantle. "I found it! Grandmother, look! I found it!" she shrieked, running for the stairs.

"Well, I suppose you did," Grandmother said. "And it was on the fireplace, just like you said it would be. But didn't we agree to wait until it's cooler?"

Rose had disappeared around the corner at the top of the main stairs and was headed for the end of the hallway. She bounded up the narrow attic stairs two at a time. As a flash of lightning lit the dark attic and a rumble of thunder shook the floor boards, she at last tried with trembling fingers to insert the key into the lock of the trunk. Grandmother appeared on the top step. "Whoo!" she puffed. "I think I'm getting too old for all this stair climbing."

The trunk was open. Rose knelt beside it, while Grandmother pulled up a wobbly stool and dropped down on it. Inside the trunk were a scrap of cloth, a pile of papers tied with a string, and an envelope containing a birthday card signed "With love from your brother." The name Tom was scrawled at the bottom.

"What is this?" Rose held a brown, leather-covered book in the gray light from the open dormer window. The book was fastened with a bright metal snap. She glanced at it and tossed it back into the trunk. "Does any of this stuff mean anything?"

Grandmother shrugged. "I suppose it once did to somebody. The key certainly was well hidden." She picked up the leather-covered book and unsnapped the flap. "It's a picture album," she said, moving her stool nearer the window.

Rose took the scrap of cloth out of the trunk and held it up. It was a dull green color and looked as if part of it had been cut away.

"Tom and me," Grandmother mumbled.

Rose suddenly realized that her grandmother had been speaking under her breath for a while. "Did you say something?"

Grandmother held the book closer to her face. "The writing under this picture says 'Tom and me.' I wonder . . . could that be Uncle Tom Evans? I heard my mother speak of him many times."

"The birthday card was signed by Tom," Rose said.

Grandmother nodded thoughtfully. "He was my mother's uncle—her mother's brother."

Rose examined the black-and-white picture. A man and a woman stood arm-in-arm in front of a blooming bush. The woman wore a hat with a wide brim. "It says 'Tom and *me.*' The trunk must have belonged to her."

"Apparently. But I can't tell who she is, the hat shades her face so." Grandmother flipped through the pages. "Undoubtedly some of these children are other aunts and uncles I've only known as adults." As she was about to close the book, a yellowed snapshot fell to the dusty attic floor. It was of a young girl standing on an expansive porch.

"That's Fineweather," Rose said.

"It sure is," Grandmother said. "The way it looked goodness knows how long ago."

"See where the picture was stuck? There is another one like it. Is it the same girl?"

"No. They look alike, but they are dressed differently. They must have taken each other's picture."

"Someone has written 'Friends 4-ever.' I wonder who they are."

Grandmother stared at the two pictures for a long time. Then she carefully put the loose one back inside the album and snapped the cover. For a long moment, she sat like a statue with the book in her lap as she stared out the window at a sliver of golden sunlight that had found its way from behind a dark, heavy cloud.

CHAPTER 5

RING

"Grandmother! Grandmother, are you all right?" Rose said.

Grandmother gave a start. She took a deep breath of the damp, fresh air that drifted through the attic window. "Yes, I'm fine." She stood up. "Now, I believe I have had all the exploring I can stand for one day. Haven't you?"

"I . . . guess so." Rose was surprised to notice that grandmother's arm was around her waist and she was being propelled gently toward the top of the stairs.

"I thought you were going to the Peabody Place today."

"You talked me out of it. It's raining."

Grandmother and Rose descended both sets of stairs and walked out on the big front porch. "But look, the rain has stopped," Grandmother said, taking a seat in a metal lawn chair on a dry part of the porch.

"It's nice and fresh after the rain, isn't it?"

"Um-hm. I love a day like this. Everything glistens so when the sun comes out right after a rain. You know, I'll bet if you stayed on the best paths you would hardly get wet at all. I have some rubber boots that might just fit you."

"What if the rain starts again?"

"Take my old raincoat." Grandmother hurried into the house and brought out the raincoat and the boots.

"I don't know if that girl would come on a day like this." Rose slipped the boots on and wrapped the coat around her shoulders. Grandmother had started back into the house. "Grandmother, why are you doing this?"

"Doing what?"

"Ever since you saw those pictures, you've been trying to get rid of me."

"Have I? I just have some things to do."

Rose peered through the front door and called to her Grandmother, who was already halfway up the stairs. "By the way, who were those girls in the pictures? Was one of them you?"

"No."

"Then who?"

"I'm not certain. Have a nice walk, dear. Be back before dark." Grandmother disappeared around the corner.

THE BOOTS made a sloshing, thumping noise as Rose trudged down the muddy path. She deliberately brushed against wet bushes and watched the gush of big drops. She was careful not to let any water splash on her glasses. Getting them clean again was a real pain.

The creek was swelled from the rain, but Rose was able to cross on the stepping stones. Climbing the soggy bank was not as easy as usual, but Rose soon found her way to the old house.

She looked through the front window before going in. No one was there. She stuck her head in the door and called, "Hello," but there was no answer. "That figures," she said. She took off the raincoat, folded it, and dropped it on the top porch step. As she sat down, she said, "If I don't find her pretty soon, I'll probably chicken out."

"You're Rosalyn, aren't you?" said a voice behind her.

Rose sprang to her feet and whirled around to find the girl in the white dress standing in the open doorway, not five feet away. Now that she was face to face with the girl, Rose wished she could run, but she couldn't.

"How do you know my name?" Rose found herself saying.

"I know a lot about you."

"Like what?"

"Your name is Rosalyn Carlisle, and you are staying with your grandmother for the summer."

"Someone must have told you about me."

"You will be moving to a new city soon, and the thought of going to a new school frightens you."

"No one could have told you *that*. I never told anyone that I'm scared. I've complained plenty, but I never said I'm scared."

"I would be scared, too, under the same circumstances."

"Do you live around here?"

"Mmm," the girl said with a shrug, which was really no answer at all.

"I was afraid you wouldn't come today— because of the weather, I mean."

"I don't mind the rain. Why are you staring at me?"

"You look familiar somehow. I mean, now that I see you up close, you look like someone I've seen before."

"You have seen me twice."

"No, there is someone else you remind me of." Rose squinted her eyes and pushed her glasses up on her nose. "Do you have a name or something?"

"Or something?"

"A name, I mean. Do you have a name?"

"My name is Ring."

"Ring? Just Ring?"

"That's it." Ring flicked a drop of water from her red hair and moved to another part of the step and sat down.

Rose sat back down on the raincoat. "So you did see me those other times. Why didn't you say something?"

"Why didn't *you*?"

"I have trouble talking to people."

"Most folks are pretty easy to talk to when you give them the chance."

"I've given them chances."

"Did you have some traumatic experience that made you afraid of people?"

"Not that I remember. I've just never been comfortable around people, that's all. Especially people my own age."

Ring laid her hands together on her lap and leaned back against the porch post. "So that's why you didn't have many friends at school."

"What you talking about? I had dozens of friends." Rose sighed. "Who am I kidding? You're right. I *knew* dozens of people, that's all. I think my brains scared them away, since none of them had any. And to make matters worse, now I'm leaving everybody I know."

Ring nodded.

"Hey," said Rose, "how do you know all this stuff about me?"

Ring shrugged without saying anything.

"Who are you anyway?" said Rose.

"I'm the friend you apparently never had."

"Why would you want to be *my* friend?"

"Why wouldn't I?"

"Believe me, I've asked myself that question a million—a *billion* times." Rose jumped up and backed away. "Wait! You're not some kind of witch doctor or a voodoo person or something, are you? Hey, I'm not selling my immortal soul to *nobody*!"

Ring's mouth twisted, and her eyes went to the gray sky overhead. "Come on. You don't believe in that junk."

"I didn't use to. But what about the way you come and go without making any noise? A ghost? Are you a ghost?"

"Don't be silly."

"Then what? My fairy godmother—er, god-sister?"

"What do you want me to be?"

"I'm not sure." Rose sat down again. "You certainly aren't an ordinary kid like me."

"Thank goodness! You have too many problems."

Just then a rumble of thunder shook the boards of the porch where Rose and Ring were sitting. Rose stood up and quickly put the raincoat on. "I hope I can make it back before the rain starts again. You want to come? Grandmother said I can have people over."

"No, thanks."

"Will you be here tomorrow?"

"Probably."

"See you, then." Rose started off through the woods and then turned to wave at Ring, who waved back from the front window of the shack. Rose stumbled over a wet tree root, and when she straightened up again, Ring was gone.

HEAVY RAIN was falling by the time Rose got to the house. Grandmother came from the hallway at the top of the stairs. She hung Rose's dripping raincoat on a rack beside the front door, and Rose kicked off her muddy boots and left them on some newspapers that Grandmother had put down for that purpose.

Grandmother went to the big chair by the fireplace and sat on the edge of it, motioning for Rose to sit across from her on the sofa. "So how did your visit go?"

"How do you know I visited anyone?"

"That's what you went out there for, wasn't it?"

"Yes, but I . . . oh, there are so many strange things going on."

"So, tell me."

"I did talk to the girl. She was at the Peabody Place, but I didn't see her at first. I like her, Grandmother. She said she wants to be my friend. Can you believe it?"

"Did you find out her name?" Grandmother seemed to perch a bit more lightly on the edge of her chair.

"She told me her name is Ring."

Grandmother let out her breath and settled back in the chair.

"Strange name, isn't it?" said Rose. "Just Ring. That's what she said."

"What else did she tell you?"

"She knew a lot about me. How could she know me? I didn't know *her*."

"Hmmm. It *is* quite a riddle."

"I can't wait to go back."

"Looks like the rain has set in for the rest of the day. Maybe tomorrow. Meanwhile, how about a bite of lunch?"

"All right." Rose bounded up the stairs two at a time. She ducked into the bathroom to wash quickly and then went to the mirror in her room to comb her hair. Suddenly she stopped. She picked her glasses up from the dresser and put them on. She took them off again and squinted at her reflection. "It's me!" she said in a breathless whisper. "That's why she looked so familiar. Ring looks like me without my glasses!"

CHAPTER 6

RING AROUND ROSE

Rose spent every possible minute at the Peabody Place or at Sand Creek. Ring was there every time Rose returned. The girls spent many hours roaming the hillsides and meadows, picking flowers, tossing stones into the water, and talking. Rose felt free to tell Ring anything. She was surprised to find that when she talked about her disappointments and fears, they didn't seem so large as they did when she kept them locked up inside.

Tuesday, June 22, 1971

"HAVE YOU changed your mind about starting at your new school?" Ring sat at the edge of the creek and splashed her bare feet in the water. "Maybe even looking forward to it?"

"Ugh!" Rose lay flat on her back, watching three buzzards soar high against the blue sky. "I haven't thought about school in weeks. Anyway, you're supposed to know stuff. You should know I'm not looking forward to it."

"Could it be all that bad?"

"How many times have *you* had to move to a big town where you don't know a soul and everyone thinks of you as a strange new kid and stares at you?"

"And how many times have *you* done that?"

"Okay, so this is my first time. But it will be awful! I just know it will be *awful!*"

"Well, there *are* a lot of unknowns, I'll grant you that, and people act pretty stupid sometimes. But maybe you could think of it as a chance to start over."

"Start over?" Rose sat up and dropped her feet into the water beside Ring's.

"That's exactly what you're doing. Look, you've gone to Mill Road all your life, and it hasn't been all that great, right?"

"All that great? It's been awful!"

"Everything's awful for you, huh?"

"Pretty much."

"Well, it's not likely that would change, no matter how long you stayed at Mill Road. But in Jonesboro, no one will know the old you."

"I will still *be* the old me. Plain old Rosalyn Kaye Carlisle, a.k.a. Rose Carlisle, smart but miserable person. I can't bear to think of all those times other kids called me 'four eyes' and made fun of me because I'm smarter than them. I'm not going to play dumb just to fit in."

"There's nothing wrong with wearing glasses. I mean, come on, you gotta see, right? And as far as being smart, that sounds to me like a *good* thing. Anyway, by the time the kids at the new school figure out how smart you are, you'll already have a lot of friends."

"That's just it. You don't understand. I can't meet new kids."

"Face it, kiddo. It's coming, whether you're ready or not."

"Do you remember the first day I met you and I said I didn't know what I wanted you to be? Well, now I know. I want you to be someone who can work magic. I'd almost settle for some voodoo. Whatever it takes to keep from having to move to Jonesboro. I'll die if I have to move to Jonesboro!"

"You're not gonna die."

Rose propped her head in her hands and gazed into the water. "It's silly, I know, so you can go ahead and laugh."

Ring didn't laugh. "You sound pretty desperate, kid. We've got to think of something." She put her finger to her chin and appeared in deep thought, her eyes shifting to the left and to the right. Then she straightened up and said, "Yep, it just might work." She jumped up and started for the Peabody Place, motioning for Rose to follow.

Rose quickly wiped her eyes beneath her glasses, then snatched up her shoes and socks and followed. When she got to the shack, Ring was scanning the big front room. She instructed Rose to help her move the ragged sofa out of the middle of the floor, which left the major portion of the room bare.

"What are you gonna do?" Rose asked.

Ring pointed to the middle of the floor. "Sit there."

Rose sat cross-legged where Ring pointed.

"Close your eyes," Ring said.

"What for?"

"Just do it."

Rose closed her eyes tightly. She could hear and feel Ring walking in a wide circle around her. "What are you doing?"

"You'll find out. Now, blot out all of your worries about the bad things you think will happen. Pay attention to the friendly faces—the teachers, the students, everyone. Are you there?"

"I'm trying."

"Now," Ring continued, still circling, "imagine that there are people around you, all smiling. Do you see them?"

"I feel sort of silly."

"This was your idea, you know."

"No, it wasn't."

"Okay, just play along."

"Okay, okay, I see all the smiling faces. Hey, one guy's kinda cute."

"Forget it! Boys are a whole 'nother ballgame."

"I'd die if he came within ten feet anyway."

"Are there any girls who look friendly?"

"A couple."

"Pick out one you would like to speak to."

"But I can't, I . . ."

"They are all smiling, Rose, all friendly."

"There is one girl. She looks my age, and she's wearing glasses, too."

"So speak to her."

"What do I say?"

"What do you think you might say to a stranger?"

"I could tell her my name."

"Go ahead."

"But there isn't anybody there."

"Rose!"

"Okay, I'm talking, I'm talking." Rose swallowed hard. "Hello, my name is Rose—er, Rosalyn, Rosalyn Carlisle."

"What's *her* name?"

"Ummm, Gloria, I think."

"Good." Ring's voice came from behind Rose this time. "Now ask her to help you find someplace—a classroom, the cafeteria."

"I just moved here, Gloria, and I don't know my way around yet," Rose said into the air. "Could you please point me to the cafeteria?"

"No, ask her to go with you."

"But I can't, I . . ."

"What?" Ring had stopped beside Rose's right knee.

Rose frowned and shook her head. "Oh!" she huffed. "Would you like to have lunch with me, Gloria?"

"Yes, of course she would. So what do you have for lunch?"

"I don't know, chicken strips or something."

"And now you've finished lunch. What are you doing next?"

"Gloria's showing me where to find my next class."

"Good. Tell her you appreciate her help and you would like to eat with her again sometime."

"Thank you for helping me, Gloria, and for having lunch with me. Could we do it again sometime? Okay, Gloria. Bye-bye, Gloria."

"Is she gone?"

"Yes."

Ring stopped circling. "That's it, then. You can open your eyes."

Rose removed her glasses, rubbed her eyes, and looked around. "You are really weird, you know that?"

Ring chuckled. "Weird is in the eye of the beholder."

"How did you make that seem so real?"

"I didn't. You did."

"Would you mind telling me what just happened?"

"You met your first new friend. See how easy it was?"

"She didn't exist," Rose said, pushing her glasses up on her nose.

"It's a start. And now all you have to do is meet someone for real."

"I'm not ready for that after one lesson."

"How many do you need?"

"About a hundred."

"You get one more. Tomorrow."

Wednesday, June 23, 1971

THE NEXT day, Rose told Ring she wanted to meet an adult.

"I thought adults weren't your problem," Ring said.

"*Everyone*'s my problem," said Rose.

Ring was thoughtful for a moment. "Okay, whatever floats your boat. Let's get started."

The routine was the same. Rose sat in the middle of the floor with her eyes closed as Ring circled around her.

"So, what's this teacher's name?" asked Ring.

"She's not a teacher. She's the librarian."

"Okay, so what's the librarian's name?"

"Mrs. Smith. No, that's too plain. Mrs. Sartain."

"It doesn't matter what her name is. Stop stalling."

"Hi, Mrs. Sartain. I'm Rosalyn Carlisle, and I'm new here. I love to read. Would you please show me where the classic fiction books are?"

"So she's helping you. What book did you find?"

"*Pride and Prejudice*."

"*Pride and Prejudice*? Who reads that kind of stuff?"

"I do. I love Jane Austen."

"Of course you would. Now, thank Mrs. Sartain for help."

"Thanks, Mrs. Sartain. I look forward to coming in again sometime."

Ring stopped circling. "Okay, you can open your eyes. How did that feel?"

"It was okay, but it still wasn't real."

"So you're ready to meet someone for real?"

"Not really. Besides which there is no one around here."

"There must be someone."

"Our nearest neighbors are relatives."

"Not good enough. Think harder."

"Well, there is that man who lives on the adjoining property, Dooley Birdsong."

"Perfect!"

"I don't want to meet him."

"He's all we have right now. Summer's not going to last forever, you know."

"I would rather just forget the whole thing."

"There you go, trying to run away again. You gonna do that all your life?"

Rose heaved a sigh of resignation.

"Tell me," Ring said, "how do we find this Dooley Birdsong?"

"All I know is, he lives east of here."

CHAPTER 7

DOOLEY BIRDSONG

Rose and Ring walked east until they came to a barbed wire fence strung on green iron posts. There was enough space under the bottom wire to permit them to slide under easily. After walking a few minutes, Ring said, "I didn't know Birdsong's place was so far away.'

"I don't think it's supposed to be." Rose peered into the forest as far as she could see, but there was no sign that anyone lived close by. "Looks like we've gone the wrong direction."

"So, fearless leader," Ring said, "where do we go from here? You haven't gotten us lost, have you?"

Rose shook her head. "We'll just follow our path back to the fence and start over.

"Well, you could use some practice doing that—starting over."

Soon Rose and Ring had reached the fence and set off through the woods in a new direction.

This time, after they had gone only a short distance, Ring suddenly stopped. "What was that?" she whispered.

"I didn't hear anything." Rose moved closer to Ring.

"Just ahead," Ring whispered as she inched forward.

Then Rose heard it too, a low growl coming from some thick bushes a few feet away. She stopped to listen, and as she did, a shaggy gray animal crept out of the brush, its head hung low and emitting a low rumble.

"What *is* that thing?" Rose said in a strained whisper. "A wolf?"

"I hope it's only a dog," Ring said. "Don't make any sudden moves."

The two girls stood perfectly still as the animal bared its teeth and watched them with gleaming yellow eyes. "What are we gonna do?" Rose said, clutching Ring's arm.

"Don't ask me," Ring replied. "It looks like he's not backing down."

Rose released her grip from Ring's arm and stepped forward. "Easy boy," she said softly. "Easy, boy. Nice dog."

The animal growled again and took a step backward. "See," Rose said over her shoulder, "his growl is worse than his bite."

Just as she finished speaking, a large figure sprang from the bushes behind the dog. The dog began barking fiercely. Rose screamed as loud as she could and covered her face, expecting to be ripped apart at any second.

"What you doin' here?" a gruff voice said.

Rose dropped her hands from her face. There was a man standing only a few feet away. He seemed as tall as a giant and large around the middle. He looked as if he hadn't shaved in days, and he carried the smell of sweat, mingled with another unpleasant odor Rose couldn't name. His khaki pants and shirt were stained and wrinkled.

In his hand, he held a rifle, which he kept pointed toward the ground.

"Hesh, Butch!" the man yelled. The dog didn't quieten. "Hesh, I said!" The dog fell silent and stood by the man's side. "I asked what you're doin' here." Large gaps showed between the man's yellow teeth. "What call you got snooping around on my property?"

"You—you're Mr. Birdsong?" Rose stammered.

"I am. And I been known to *shoot* trespassers."

"We're not trespassers."

"They's a bob wire fence back yonder says you are."

"My grandmother owns the land on the other side of the fence."

Dooley Birdsong seemed to relax a little. "Elizabeth McGowan your granny, is she?"

"You know her?"

"Heard of her."

"I'm Rose, uh, Rosalyn Carlisle, and my friend Ring—" she tried to swallow a lump in her throat as she looked around "—she's here somewhere. We came to visit you."

"I ain't the visiting kind."

"We thought you might be lonesome, since you live all by yourself."

"Don't done it. I got Butch." He nodded toward the dog, who gazed up at his owner. Saliva dripped from the dog's tongue. "He's all the company I need."

"Don't you want to hear a human voice once in a while?"

"If I did, I'd get a new bat'ry for my reddio."

Rose moved closer, and as she did, she saw a peculiar bulge in Birdsong's shirt pocket. It was the shape of a small glass bottle, the black cap showing beneath the unbuttoned pocket flap.

"Look here, girl," Birdsong said. "I been on my own prit-near all my life, and I get along just fine." He waved his rifle toward the west. "Now I 'spect you and this here friend of your'n, whoever she is, best get on back to where you come from."

"We were trying to be nice to you," Rose said, a little angry now that her fear was subsiding. Birdsong didn't look nearly as large as he had earlier.

"Well, you run along and be nice to somebody else."

Rose's head told her to run, but her feet felt stuck to the ground. "But—"

"No buts!" Birdsong snapped, baring his ugly teeth and stomping his foot, which started Butch to barking again. "Now you *git!* 'Less you want a load of buckshot in that behind or a plug bit out of it by this here wolf-dog." He raised the rifle into the air as if he were about to pull the trigger, but he didn't. "I said *git*, and I mean *git!*"

As Butch continued to yap crazily, Rose broke loose and headed for the fence. She hit the ground on her belly and cleared the barbed wire without slowing down. When she neared the Peabody shack, Ring was standing in the doorway.

"Why did you abandon me?" Rose said breathlessly as she fell on the dirty couch. "You left me out there with that maniac!"

"I can't help you all the time, you know."

"You sure helped me get into that!" Rose jerked off her glasses and wiped sweat from her face with the tail of her shirt. "Some friend *you* turned out to be!" She slapped her glasses back on and tucked her hair behind her ears.

"I really think that old man was bluffing," Ring said. "Just like his mangy dog."

"Well, they did a good job of convincing *me*. And if you think I'm going back over there, you're not just weird, you're crazy."

"Much as I hate to admit it, you're probably right—about not going back over there, I mean."

CHAPTER 8

PETAL

Thursday, June 24, 1971

Asliver of sunlight found its way between the curtains and struck Rose in the face. She blinked and slid out of bed, then went to the window and opened the curtains. Down below, on a trellis next to the porch, some red roses nodded in the hot morning breeze. A cicada droned in a nearby tree, and a robin bobbed along the ground, head cocked to one side, looking for breakfast.

Catching the odor of sizzling bacon, Rose shed her night gown and pulled on her jeans, T-shirt, and tennis shoes. She grabbed her glasses from the dresser and hurried down the stairs to the kitchen.

"You're up early today," Grandmother said over a cup of coffee.

Rose washed her hands at the sink and sat down at the table without saying anything.

"Big plans?" Grandmother asked.

"Not really."

"Are you going to visit Ring today?"

"Um-hm."

"What's the matter?"

"Nothing."

"Is there something you want to tell me?"

"Not really."

"Something you *don't* want to tell me?" When Rose still didn't answer, Grandmother said, "My, but you're stingy with words this morning."

Rose began to eat. "Grandmother," she said, pausing between bites, "do you think there is some good in everybody?"

"I should hope so. It would be sad, don't you think, for someone to be rotten to the core?"

"But aren't there people like that?"

"I suppose there are." Grandmother set her cup down and gave Rose a concerned look. "You and Ring are getting along okay, aren't you?"

"Oh, yes, she's the best."

Grandmother's brow furrowed, but she didn't ask any more questions. "I read your mother's letter again a while ago. The new house sounds nice."

"Yes, it does."

"Will you have her come for you now, as she suggested?"

"I want to stay here the rest of the summer. That is, if you don't mind."

"Nothing would please me more. You'll need to let her know, though."

"I'll write Mom soon."

AFTER ROSE and Grandmother had cleared away the breakfast dishes, Rose set out for her daily visit to the Peabody Place. She had just slammed the screen door and sprang off the back porch when her foot struck something soft. There was a sharp yelp as something small and white rolled between her feet. She gave a startled screech and tumbled to the ground. Then she sat up and looked at the shaggy ball of fur. "Well, hello there," she said, surprised.

Grandmother appeared at the door. "What is it?"

"I tripped—over that. Look, Grandmother, it's a dog."

"So it is." Grandmother stepped out and examined the animal closer.

"She's beautiful! Grandmother, may I keep her?"

"Don't you suppose she belongs to someone?" Grandmother patted the little dog's head, trying in vain to avoid the pink tongue that was determined to do some licking. She dusted her hands together. "And I'd say she's a bit ragged to be called beautiful."

"I think she's beautiful," Rose said, hugging the dog to her breast. The dog stretched up and licked Rose's face. "If I give her a bath and trim her hair, then may I keep her?"

"I suppose it wouldn't hurt until we find out who she belongs to."

"It looks like she hasn't belonged to anyone in a long time. Maybe she was abandoned. In which case, she needs a good home."

"She'll have to stay outside. And of course, your folks will decide whether she goes home with you. Meanwhile, she's your responsibility."

Rose brushed the thick fur from the dog's big brown eyes and hugged her again. "I'll take good care of her."

After feeding the dog some gravy left over from breakfast, Rose began working over her new pet. She used an old pair of garden shears for the haircut, which was a tedious task, since the fur was so thick and matted.

Grandmother sat under a shade tree, fanning herself with a folded newspaper. "So, what are you going to call her?"

"I've been thinking about that. She's pretty as a flower and not much bigger, so I am going to call her Flower. No, that's not it. Petal—that's what I'll call her. Her name is Petal."

"That's nice. It sort of goes along with your name—Rose and Petal."

When the haircut was finished, Rose found a place in the hot sun to fill a tub with soapy water. Both Rose and Petal had such a good time that the bath took much longer than necessary.

As Petal lay in the sun to dry, Grandmother patted her on the head. "I must say, Miss Petal, you certainly look better than you did this morning."

"She sure does," said Rose. "I can't wait to show her to . . . oh, my goodness! I had no idea this would take so long. Ring must wonder what's happened to me!"

"You'll have time for a visit this afternoon."

WHEN ROSE set out after lunch, Petal followed right at her heels. Ring wasn't at their favorite spot by the creek. When they got to the shack, they found it vacant. Rose called, but there was no answer.

Petal made a quick search of the Peabody Place and then returned to Rose's side. "I wonder where she is," Rose said to Petal. "Maybe her folks wouldn't let her come today. I guess she has folks. She doesn't talk about them."

At the creek, Rose sat on a rock and skipped flat stones across the water. Petal seemed to be interested, so Rose tossed a twig along the bank for Petal to chase. She threw it again and watched delightedly as Petal bounded after it.

From then on, Petal waited every morning on the back steps until Rose appeared. Then she would take her place beside Rose and follow her to the Peabody Place, the creek, the meadow, or wherever Rose cared to go. Rose hoped Ring would be there every day; but when she wasn't, there was always something to do anyway.

Friday, July 2, 1971

IT WAS another white-hot morning, and Rose swung out the back door, letting the screen slam behind her. Petal wasn't waiting. Rose called repeatedly, but Petal didn't come. Rose circled the house twice, peering beneath the bushes against the house, where Petal often lay to cool off, but there was no trace of her.

Grandmother stepped into the sunlight on the porch, wiping her face with a damp cloth. "Where's Petal?"

"That's what I'd like to know. I'm afraid something's happened to her."

"Maybe she went to the Peabody Place ahead of you."

"She never goes without me," Rose said, her throat becoming tight.

"Maybe this time."

Rose ran toward the woods, calling Petal's name the entire way. As she neared the shack, Ring glanced out the window and then came out onto the porch.

"Where have you been?" Rose said, leaping up the creaking steps toward the front door. "I've looked for you every day."

"You haven't really looked for me."

"Yes, I have, I . . ." Rose put her hand to her lips. "I haven't, have I? I'm sorry, Ring. I guess I've been preoccupied. You see, I have a—"

"A little white dog."

"You *would* know, wouldn't you? I've lost her, and I have to find her. Is she inside?" Rose started past Ring toward the door of the shack.

Ring grabbed Rose's arm. "Wait. There's something I have to tell you."

Rose started for the door again. "So tell me."

"Rose, *wait!*" Ring insisted, tugging harder on Rose's arm.

Rose wrenched away from Ring's grasp and barged through the door. "What is with you? I haven't even seen you in days, and now all of a sudden you act like . . . ." She stopped when she saw what lay on a tattered sofa cushion beneath the window. "Petal!" she screamed, running to where the lifeless form lay stretched on the torn fabric. Spots of blood were splattered on Petal's curly white fur.

"I tried to stop you," Ring said. "I didn't want you to find out this way."

"Petal! Oh, no! Petal!" Rose cried, grabbing the dog up in her arms. "Wake up, Petal! Please, Petal, please don't be dead!" Petal didn't move. Enormous sobs racked Rose's body as Ring sat on the floor beside her.

"But—but *why?*" Rose wailed. "What happened?"

"All I know is I found her like this over near the Birdsong property. It looks as if something attacked her."

"Attacked her? No! No! Petal never hurt anyone. Only a cruel, vicious killer could have done this." Rose raised her head quickly, her face streaked with dirty tears. "It was that wolf-dog, wasn't it?" Ring didn't answer. "*Wasn't it?!*" Rose shouted.

"There's no way to know for sure. There were larger animal tracks nearby."

The heartache that Rose had felt now became seething anger. "Then I'm going to kill *it!*"

"You can't," Ring protested. "It might kill you first."

"I won't give it the chance." Rose carefully laid Petal's limp body on the cushion and started for the door.

"Then you'll make Mr. Birdsong mad and he'll shoot you."

"I don't care! Get out of my way!" Rose rushed out into the woods and grabbed a heavy stick. "You coming or not?"

Ring followed empty-handedly.

CHAPTER 9

WOLF HUNT

Soon Rose and Ring were hiding in a thicket, from which they could see a rickety shanty that stood in the clearing. The shanty was covered in weathered green siding and had a rusty tin roof, above which a bent stove pipe reached toward the sky. A few weeds grew here and there, and sunlight glinted off tin cans that littered the yard. Behind the shanty was a small garbage heap. It wasn't clear where the yard ended and the heap began.

The space between Rose and the shack was only about 50 feet, but it may as well have been 50 miles. Rose looked at the club she held in her hand and then back at the shanty. "Who am I kidding?" she said to Ring. "I can't do it." She dropped to her knees and was about to break into sobs when she heard heavy footsteps behind her.

She jumped up and whirled around to see Mr. Birdsong and Butch standing not ten feet away.

Birdsong was wearing the sweat-soaked khaki clothes he always wore, and the band of his crumpled hat was wringing wet. The stench of sweat and wet dog hung heavy in the still afternoon air. Butch stood stiff-legged with his head down, his dripping tongue lolling almost to the ground, as he waited for a command from his master.

Rose was trapped. If she ran, Butch was sure to chase her.

Birdsong wasn't carrying his rifle, but in his left hand he held one of his glass bottles. For an endless moment, he stood staring at Rose with red, unblinking eyes. Finally, he spoke. "I thought I made it plain you ain't welcome here."

As Rose's fear began to rise, so did her anger. "I've come for *him*," she said, pointing at Butch.

"Butch?" Birdsong half shut one eye and glared at Rose with the other. "Butch ain't for sale."

Rose knew she was in over her head, but she couldn't seem to stop herself. "I don't want to buy him. I want to *kill* him."

Birdsong's head jerked sideways stupidly. "Kill him? Kill old Butch, ye say?"

"You heard me."

"Mind if I ask what fer?"

"He killed my Petal. She was just a helpless little dog, and that mangy animal killed her."

Birdsong was silent for a moment, as if trying to decide whether to take Rose seriously. Then he said, "Got proof of that, do ye?"

"I have . . ." Rose's voice cracked, and a lump swelled in her throat. She swallowed hard and blundered on. "I have a dead dog."

"And this here dog of your'n told you before it expired, did it, that Butch was the one done it?"

"I just know he did it!"

"Supposin' he did. Killing Butch ain't gonna change nothing."

"Petal's killer doesn't deserve to live."

Butch sensed that something was wrong. He began to inch toward Rose, a low rumble emanating from his throat. Rose picked the club up from where she had dropped it, fearing that she was about to need it after all.

"Easy, girl," Birdsong said. "You get Butch riled up, no telling what he'll do."

Her heart thumping wildly, Rose drew the club back to defend herself from the approaching animal. Birdsong lunged for the club, and when he got close enough, Rose landed a swift kick on his shin. He let out a yelp and grabbed for her, but he tripped over Butch, sprawled headlong, and struck his head on the dry, hard ground.

Butch barked a few times, and then, realizing his master was in trouble, slunk over and started to lick Birdsong's whiskery face. Birdsong began to thrash about on the ground. Relieved that Birdsong wasn't hurt too badly, Rose took the opportunity to get away quickly.

After the ordeal, Rose and Ring both collapsed on the cushionless sofa at the Peabody Place. Rose mopped her brow with the tail of her shirt.

"Your grandmother's bound to find out about your visit with Mr. Birdsong," Ring said. "You need to make sure she hears your side first."

"You're probably right. Anyway, I'll have to tell her what happened to Petal."

Rose opened the old trunk and lovingly placed Petal's lifeless body on top of the papers and shut the lid. After carrying the trunk outside, Rose and Ring pried loose boards from the porch and used the jagged ends to dig a hole beneath a big oak tree behind the shack. At last, they were able to drop the trunk gently into the hole and cover it with dirt."

Rose heaved a sigh and pushed her glasses up on her nose. "Will you be here tomorrow?" she asked Ring.

"I'm all you got now. I'll be here."

CHAPTER 10

THE FIRE

Rose managed to sneak up to her room to take a quick shower and change clothes before she had to confront her grandmother. When she came back down, Grandmother was chopping something at the stove.

"Rose, what on earth is wrong?" Grandmother said, looking up from her work. "Have you been crying?"

Rose tried to speak matter-of-factly, but her voice wavered as she said, "Petal is dead."

"Dead?" Grandmother left the stove and sat down at the table across from Rose.

"Ring found her out by the fence near the Birdsong property. We buried her at the Peabody Place today. I think Mr. Birdsong's wolf-dog killed her."

"Wolf-dog?"

"It's an ugly gray thing, and I hate it."

"You've seen it?"

Rose nodded, keeping her face toward the floor. "A couple of times." She wasn't ready to tell Grandmother about this afternoon's wolf hunt.

"Dooley Birdsong must be the one you were asking me about then."

Rose nodded again. "And now I know that people *can* be rotten to the core, like you said. *He* is. And so is his dog."

"Then you'll stay away from him. I want you to never go near his place again."

Rose continued to stare at the floor.

"I think I'll give Sheriff Tate a call after supper and see if he has had other complaints on Dooley Birdsong or his dog."

"I'm not hungry, Grandmother. If you don't mind, I think I'll go up to my room now."

"Suit yourself, dear."

Rose dragged herself up the stairs. Tired as she was, sleep didn't come until the wee hours of the morning.

Saturday, July 3, 1971

WHEN SHE awoke, the clock on the nightstand showed 10:30 a.m. She forced herself up slowly, got dressed, and went downstairs to find her grandmother waiting in the living room.

"Did you sleep well, dear?" Grandmother asked.

"Not really."

Grandmother patted the couch beside her. "Sit down. I need to talk to you."

Rose sat. "What's wrong, Grandmother?"

"Rose, did you leave the house after you excused yourself from supper last evening?"

"No."

"You wouldn't lie to me."

"Of course not. What is it?"

"I called Sheriff Tate last night, like I said. He has received no complaints about our neighbor or his wolf-dog, as you call it. Then, this morning, the sheriff called *me*." Grandmother paused and fixed her gray eyes straight into Rose's. "There was a fire at Birdsong's place last night. His shack burned to the ground."

Rose's mouth fell open. "And you think *I* did it?"

"He says you did. He insists that you are the only one around here who would want to do him harm."

"I didn't go over there last night."

"But you did go over there yesterday. You made threats against his dog."

Rose studied her hands, which lay limply in her lap. "I'm sorry, Grandmother. I just couldn't tell you."

"He said you kicked him."

"I did, but just to get away from him. He came at me first."

"Mr. Birdsong is convinced that you would have done anything to get even with him. According to him, you sneaked over there and started the fire while he was asleep. He claims he was lucky to get out alive."

"And you believe him?"

"I don't know what to believe. I do know how upset you were over losing Petal, and I can imagine how angry you must have felt."

"I still feel it! I hate that animal! And I hate that man!"

"Oh, Rose! Hate is a powerful emotion. It makes people do terrible things."

"I didn't start any fire. Grandmother, please believe me. I didn't go out last night, and I would never set fire to anybody's house."

A look of relief swept across Grandmother's face, and her shoulders relaxed as if a weight had been lifted from them. "I believe you, dear. Please forgive me for being so harsh. Our family is respected in this community, and I want to keep it that way."

"What are we going to do?"

"Lucky for us, Hollis Tate and I go back a long way. He knows I will tell him the truth. But how on earth will we convince Dooley Birdsong? A man like that doesn't trust anybody."

"He sure doesn't give anyone reason to trust *him* either."

Grandmother shook her head. "Distrust breeds distrust. It's a vicious cycle. That poor man!"

"He's not likely to break the cycle himself."

"You're probably right about that."

Rose settled back on the sofa. "I wonder if someone else could break the cycle."

"Who would it be?"

Rose was silent for a moment, and then an idea began to form. "Looks like I'm the one who stands to gain the most by winning his good will."

"You already tried to make friends with him, and he treated you terribly."

"Maybe if I tried a different angle." She tapped her chin with her finger, the way she had seen Ring do. "What does Mr. Dooley Birdsong need most right now?"

"Right now, the poor man needs a place to stay."

"Exactly. And I know just the place."

"You do?"

"The Peabody Place, where else?"

"I suppose it would be all right for a while."

"Of course, it belongs to Ring and me, but—"

"Oh?"

"Well, it sort of does. Only right now he needs it more than we do."

"It might be worth a try. The poor man is probably wondering where he will spend the night."

"Grandmother, I wish you would stop calling him 'poor man.' He's a despicable liar, and he's trying to frame me."

Grandmother went to the phone and called the Sheriff, then returned to the living room. "Mr. Birdsong happened to be in the sheriff's office. They're on their way over here right now."

WHEN THE black-and-white car pulled up outside, Rose peeked out the curtain and then went to the far side of the living room. Grandmother glanced at Rose, took a deep breath, and went to answer the knock.

"Morning, Elizabeth," said Sheriff Tate, removing his hat to reveal thin, grayish hair.

"Good morning, Hollis," Grandmother said. "And you must be Mr. Birdsong. I'm Elizabeth McGowan." She offered her hand, and Dooley Birdsong touched it as if it were red hot. "Do come in," Grandmother continued. "I'm so pleased to finally meet you." Birdsong nodded without a word and made no effort to remove his floppy, sweat-stained hat. His eyes darted from one side of the big hallway to the other, as if trying to take it all in at once. If Grandmother noticed any disagreeable odors, she didn't let on.

After directing the two men into the parlor, Grandmother motioned toward Rose, who stood almost hidden behind a high-backed chair. "This is my granddaughter Rose. You remember my daughter Sarah, don't you, Hollis? Rose is her daughter. I understand that Rose and Mr. Birdsong have already met."

Grandmother asked the two men to sit, which they did, Mr. Birdsong spreading himself over half the couch and the sheriff parking his tall frame on a footstool near the cold hearth.

"Say, Elizabeth, you've really fixed this place up," the sheriff said. "I've never seen Fineweather looking better."

"Thank you, Hollis. It's been a challenge, but one I've enjoyed. Now, could I get you gentlemen something to drink? Perhaps some iced tea would be fitting on a morning like this."

The sheriff looked at Mr. Birdsong, whose sour expression didn't change. "Some of your famous sweet tea would be nice, Elizabeth," Sheriff Tate said.

"I'll get it," Rose said quickly, not wanting to be left alone with the visitors. When she returned, Grandmother was saying something about the Peabody Place.

"I don't want no charity," Mr. Birdsong said gruffly. He shot a mean look at Rose as she set the tinkling glasses on the table in front of him.

"Still yet, it *was* your granddaughter burned me out last night." Grandmother and Sheriff Tate exchanged a look but both managed to hold their tongues.

Rose quickly backed away. She suddenly remembered how much she despised Dooley Birdsong.

"So you'll take Mrs. McGowan up on her kind offer will you, Dooley?" Sheriff Tate asked, just before taking a long drink from his glass.

"I figure it's the least they can do after what that young'n done to me," Birdsong said.

The sheriff was unable to hold his peace this time. "Now, Dooley, I advise you to keep quiet about that. You know as well as I do you got no proof."

"I got a burned house."

Anger gave Rose the courage to speak. "And your house told you before it burned all the way down that I was the one who set it afire?"

The room fell silent as Mr. Birdsong's eyes met Rose's, and for a moment his expression seemed to soften. He looked toward the floor and then up again. He drained his glass with one last gulp and rose to leave. "Much obliged for the drink," he said, turning for the door.

"By the way, Elizabeth," Sheriff Tate said, "you might be interested to know that I'm holding Dooley's rifle until this is all settled. He says he has a license for it, but so far I haven't been able to verify that."

"That's just as well while he is staying on my land," Grandmother said. "And may I make one more request? While you live out there, would you please confine your dog. I don't like it threatening my granddaughter."

"Butch don't take to being shut up," Mr. Birdsong said.

"It's not too much to ask," said the sheriff.

Birdsong looked from Mrs. McGowan to Rose and back to the sheriff, then left without saying anything else.

"Thanks, Elizabeth," the sheriff said, stepping out on the front porch. "If anything surfaces, I'll let you know."

"I'd appreciate that, Hollis. And Mr. Birdsong, I hope you get along fine at the Peabody Place."

"Reckon I will," Birdsong grumbled. "I've lived in worse."

The shack that burned down was worse, Rose wanted to say, but she kept quiet as the sheriff's car pulled away.

"Now, that wasn't so bad," Grandmother said, returning to the living room. "What was that you said about his house speaking to him before it burned?"

"That's what he said to me yesterday. He asked if Petal told me that it was his dog that killed her."

"What a dreadful thing for him to say!"

"The difference is, I didn't burn his house, but Butch *did* kill Petal."

"Now, just as the sheriff told Mr. Birdsong, I'm telling *you*, you have no real proof. I suggest you be careful what you say. It was your idea to help him."

"Only for a short time—hopefully a *very* short time. And only to get him to drop the case against me." Rose shook herself as if trying to waken from a bad dream. "I'm not sure I can do it."

"You can, and you must. Be thankful he settled so easily. If he is truly convinced you burned his house, he could make things pretty rough on you."

"I don't want him to think I did that."

"Then somehow he has to be convinced otherwise."

CHAPTER 11

THE PLAN

Monday, July 5, 1971

Rose didn't visit Ring on Sunday, the day after Mr. Birdsong moved into the Peabody Place, as the church had a picnic to celebrate July 4. That was just as well, because Grandmother thought it best that she stay away until Mr. Birdsong and his dog were settled. On Monday, Rose set out early and found Ring down by the creek.

"So is this where you stay now?" Rose asked Ring.

"Uh . . . no, I don't stay out here," Ring replied, brushing imaginary dust from the front of her white dress.

"So where *do* you live?"

"It's quite a ways from here."

"You enjoy being mysterious, don't you?"

"Are you allowed to visit Mr. B. today?"

"I suppose so. I have to be nice to him, even if it kills me, which it probably will."

When Rose and Ring neared the old house, smoke was rising from the chimney and the door and windows were wide open. "I don't see the wolf-dog," Rose whispered.

Ring shook her head. "He must be inside."

Rose removed her glasses and wiped sweat from her eyes. "Whew! How can he stand to cook on a day like this?" As she neared the steps, Dooley Birdsong appeared at the front door, eyeing her suspiciously. Butch stood inside, peering out between Mr. Birdsong's knees.

Birdsong didn't speak as he stepped onto the porch, blocking the door so Butch couldn't get out. The dry boards creaked under his weight. He pulled a red bandanna from his hip pocket and patted his bristly face.

Rose finally found her voice. "Um, my grandmother said if you need anything, let her know. She—I mean, *we* are awfully sorry about what happened to your house."

"Well, sorry don't change nothing." He flicked his hand at Rose, as if shooing away a fly. "And I don't need nothing else from your granny."

Rose swallowed hard and blundered on. "Look, Mr. Birdsong, we are trying to be neighborly. No matter what you think, I did not set fire to your house." Birdsong's expression didn't change. "Won't you just believe me? Can't we be friends?"

"Like I told you before, girl, I don't need no friends. And I don't like nobody snooping around."

Rose wanted to remind him that this was not his property and he couldn't run her off this time, but Birdsong's stare and the two yellow eyes glaring out between his knees were beginning to get to her. She started to back away slowly.

"Well, I guess I'll be going then," she said as calmly as possible. She forced herself to walk up the path toward the woods. Looking back, she saw that Butch had followed a few yards, sniffing at the tracks her sneakers had left in the dust. When she was certain she was out of sight, she broke into a run. Ring was sitting near the creek on a pad of soft green moss.

"So, what do you do now?" Ring asked.

"You got me," Rose said with a shrug. "That's one tough nut to crack. And I do mean *nut*. But I can't go on being nice to that man forever. And I refuse to be made to feel guilty for a crime I didn't commit." She took a seat beside Ring, slipped off her shoes and socks, and felt the cool water on her on feet. "Say, Ring, I've been thinking. What do you suppose did cause the fire at Mr. Birdsong's shack?"

"If we knew the answer to that, it would take a lot of pressure off you, wouldn't it?'

"What say we mosey over there and see what we can find?"

"Do you think we should?"

"Probably not. Grandmother said not to go out there anymore. But with Mr. Birdsong on *this* side of the fence now, I don't see what it would hurt."

"I'm with you," Ring said.

THERE WAS little left of Birdsong's shanty. A small section of the brown-shingled roof was all that was left hanging, and the smell of charred wood and scorched fabric hung in the heavy summer air. The piles of trash looked the same as before. Luckily, the grass was worn away all around the house, which probably had kept the fire from spreading to the woods. Near where the front door had been was a chunk of blackened plastic, which might have served as a curtain. Shattered glass was everywhere.

In the middle of the rubble was a clear spot where the cast-iron stove still stood with its pipe sticking into the air. "The fire had to come from this stove," Rose said.

"That seems logical." Ring used a stick to turn over a blackened board. "But how did it get out?"

Rose probed cautiously through the rubble, knocking debris out of her path with a charcoal-covered stick. A sooty skillet still sat on top of the stove, and one of the round inserts that served as a burner was leaning to one side.

She picked up a chunk of blackened material that lay on top of the stove. "Glass," she said, handing it to Ring.

"But not the same as from the window."

"No, it's thicker." Rose looked beneath the stove. "And it's scattered everywhere."

"Maybe it's a drinking glass that was broken in the fire."

Rose stooped to pick up another piece. "But look at this."

Ring turned the piece of glass over in her hand. "It has a screw top. Like the top of a bottle. There is something melted on it."

"Exactly what I thought. Like the bottle Mr. Birdsong carried in his pocket. Goodness knows what was in it. If he got too close to the fire . . ."

"If it exploded, he would have been injured."

"What if he dropped it?"

"How you gonna prove that?"

Rose tapped her chin and looked around. "First, we look for another bottle. There's bound to be more, though finding one will be like looking for a needle in a haystack—er, trash heap. You take the front. I'll take the back."

In the main dump, several yards behind the house, Rose found a collection of bottles like the ones Mr. Birdsong carried. "Here!" she shouted, and Ring came running. Rose picked up one of the bottles, unscrewed the cap and sniffed. "Phew!" she said, puckering up her face. "How could anyone drink that stuff?" She held the bottle toward Ring's nose.

"No, thanks," Ring said, pushing the bottle away.

"Now," said Rose, "let's go back and search through the burned lumber of the shack."

"What are we looking for?"

"I don't know yet. Just let me know if you find anything."

"Rose," Ring said, "I don't know if we ought to be doing this."

"So who's gonna do it? The sheriff would never buy it without proof. It's my word against Birdsong's."

Ring thrust a stick beneath a large board and lifted. "Here's a scorched sack that looks like it has sugar in it. And a can of something. The label's burned off."

"This is the place then. Keep looking."

"But what—"

"Aha!" Rose shouted triumphantly, holding up a half-empty syrup bottle. She opened the bottle she had found in the dump and poured the syrup into it. Then she held the filled bottle up to the sunlight. "Now I ask you, if you didn't know better, what would you think was in this little old bottle?"

"It does look like the real thing—whatever the real thing is."

"Now, come on. We have to pay Mr. B. another visit. I may just be able to talk him into confessing that he's the one who started that fire."

CHAPTER 12

THE CONFESSION

As Rose and Ring neared the Peabody Place, Rose noticed that there was still smoke coming from the chimney. She hid the bottle in the front of her shirt.

"You're in luck," Ring said. "Butchy boy's tied to a porch post." Butch had heard voices and was tugging at the end of his rope. When Rose stepped out of the shadows, Butch began to bark.

"Thanks, Butch old boy," Rose said. "That's just what I need to get your master's attention."

Dooley Birdsong's hulking frame appeared in the open doorway. When he saw Rose, his face twisted in a look of disgust. Butch shut up long enough to check his master's reaction to the intruder, and then, apparently satisfied he was doing the right thing, started barking again.

"Wait, Mr. Birdsong," Rose said. "Before you say anything, I have to tell you something." She glanced behind her as if she thought she were being followed. "But we don't have much time."

"What you up to, girl?"

"I have to come inside so nobody will see me." Rose looked back over her shoulder.

"I done told you a dozen times, I don't want—"

"You don't understand. I'll explain if you let me come inside. But you have to call off your dog." Rose glanced toward the woods again. "We have to hurry."

Mr. Birdsong's curiosity was aroused. "Hesh, Butch!" he shouted. Butch gave one last bark and disappeared under the porch. "All right," Mr. Birdsong said. "But no funny business, ye hear?"

"I hear." Rose followed Mr. Birdsong into the shack. She left the door open in case she had to exit quickly. The heat from the fireplace hit her like a blow torch. The air smelled of sizzling meat, dirt, and sweat. Birdsong sat on the worn couch, and Rose stood as close to the fire as she could without getting scorched.

"Look," she began, "I know you think I set fire to your shack, but I didn't. And to prove that I'm trying to be a friend, I've come to warn you." So far, so good. Birdsong seemed to be buying it. "The sheriff's on his way here right now, and I've come to tell you to hide any of those bottles you may have lying around. I'll bet you don't want him to find out about them."

Birdsong's hand went to the bulge in his shirt pocket. Then his bloodshot eyes flickered toward a brown paper sack that sat in a corner. "What makes you think I got anything to hide?"

"I put two and two together. And I just happened to find one of these over at your place." She produced the bottle from beneath her shirt.

"You been snooping around my property! You little—"

"I had to find a way to prove my innocence. And I think this is it." Holding the bottle out to the side, Rose moved closer to the fire.

Birdsong sprang from his seat. "What you gonna do, girl?"

"I'm not gonna do anything if you agree to drop the charges against me."

"I'm not dropping nothing," Birdsong said angrily. "So you best hand over that bottle and get on out of here."

"I'll leave when you confess to burning down your own shack. When you agree to tell my grandmother that you're living on her property under false pretenses."

"You're crazy!"

"Crazy enough to toss this bottle into the fire," Rose said in a desperate attempt to maintain control of the situation.

"Get away from that fire, you little imp!" Birdsong headed toward Rose.

"Don't come any closer," Rose said. "Unless you want me to toss this bottle."

Birdsong stopped. "No! No! You don't want this place to go up in flames like mine did, do you?"

"Just what's in these little bottles of yours?"

"That ain't none of your dadburned business. But let me tell you, it ain't nothing you want in that fire no more'n I do, believe me. I've had my fill of fires. Now get away from there." Heavy beads of sweat were dripping from Birdsong's face.

"And then you'll tell the sheriff how you dropped one of these bottles on your stove and started the fire?"

"Where'd you get that idea?"

"You were so drunk you couldn't stand up, and you staggered into the stove and the bottle broke into the flame."

Mr. Birdsong fixed his red eyes on Rose for a silent moment. Then the corners of his mouth quivered and his fat belly began to bounce. Soon his whole body was shaking amidst harsh laughter. "Is that—aha, ha, ha—is that what you think? I was drunk and fell on the stove?"

"It's true, isn't it?"

Mr. Birdsong stopped laughing. His face took on a look of great sobriety as he began to speak deliberately and calmly. "Now this ain't none of your business, just like I said, but seeing's how your granny has been so kind as to grant me use of this place, I'm duty bound to explain." He motioned toward the couch, but Rose didn't move. "Come on," he continued. "I heard what you said, and I can't have nobody thinking such terrible bad things about me. It's time for you to know the truth. Now, come away from there, child. Sit down and listen."

Rose left the fire. She tried to ignore the layer of gray dog hairs that coated the rough upholstery of the couch. Birdsong plopped down on the other end of the couch, panting heavily. He took out his red bandanna and mopped his face and neck.

"You see, little'n," he began, "what you don't know is, I ain't no drunkard. That ain't liquor in them bottles. That's my medicine."

"Medicine?"

"Oh, ye-ah." He shook his head, causing his chins to wiggle like jelly. "I'm a sick man, a very sick man." He put his hand on his left side. "It's my liver." His voice was almost a whisper. He slid his hand to the right side and then to his belly, as if searching for something. "I got a baaad liver."

He was rubbing his fat belly now with both hands. "The doc up in St. Louis, where I come from, he gimme six months to live. Just six months, you understand."

"Really?" Rose said, her eyes wide.

"Ye-ah. That's why I bought that little shack out yonder, humble as it was." He leaned his head to one side, and his voice became a whine. "So's I could live out my final days in peace. That's why I didn't want no company, see. Just wanted to be let alone, that's all. So's me and Butch could live in peace the last few days before I go to my final reward." His eyes drifted toward the ceiling, as if his final reward might come at any moment.

"Oh, my," Rose said. "I didn't mean to bother you in your last days."

"I know you didn't, honey, I know you didn't. But you *was* bothering me."

"And you take a lot of medicine?"

"Oh, ye-ah." His chins shook again. "It's all that keeps me going. The doc just gimme eight month's supply."

"I thought you said *six* months."

"Well, he gimme extra just in case I hung on longer."

"And the fire?"

"The fire . . . ." Birdsong's breath was coming in short gasps now, and his red bandanna had just about reached its saturation point. "Well—well, I was taking my medication—it's all that keeps me going, you understand—and I didn't see what I was doing." He leaned forward and whispered, as if he were afraid someone might overhear. Rose felt like waving his breath away. "The doc said my eyesight would be the first thing to go. Butch was laying there on the floor where he always does, and I stepped on his poor old tail. Naturally, he jumped up a-yelping, and I run over him."

"And dropped the bottle on the stove."

"Uh . . . that's right, honey. I dropped the bottle on the stove. And this here's powerful stuff. Has to be to keep me going, bad off as I am. That fire was out of hand before I knowed it."

"Why did you blame it on me?"

"You had me pretty upset coming along with that *friend* business of your'n. I was afraid my weak heart couldn't stand much more."

"You said you have a bad liver."

"Huh? Oh, I got a bad heart, too. Bad liver, bad heart. Anyways, I knowed they'd never pin nothing on you, and I hoped your granny would keep you away." He was whining again. "So's I could live out my last few days in peace."

"What's Butch gonna do when you, you know, go to your final reward?"

"I try not to think about that." Birdsong glanced toward the open door and then spoke in a very quiet voice. "He don't even know I'm a goin', poor old thang."

"Did he kill Petal?"

"I didn't witness no such tragedy. To be truthful, Butch wanders off sometimes. And my eyes being what they are these days, if he *was* gone, I might not a knowed it. Irregardless what happened to your little dog, I'm just mighty sorry, sugar."

"You'll tell the sheriff and my grandmother what you told me?"

"Lord knows I ain't looking for no sympathy, but I reckon this time I got no choice." Birdsong went to a window and looked out. Then he squinted one eye and peered back at Rose with the other. "Seems like the sheriff ought to be getting here by now, seein's how you said he's on his way."

"The sheriff's not coming. I lied about that."

"He ain't?"

"And that stuff in the bottle—it's just syrup."

"Syrup?" He picked up the bottle and smelled the cap. His face flushed, and for a second Rose thought he was going to erupt again, as she had seen him do several times before. She glanced at the open door to make sure there was a clear path if she had to run. For once, Birdsong managed to control any anger he might have felt. "And you say the sheriff nor your granny neither don't know you're here."

Rose shook her head.

"Then I reckon you best go fetch 'em, while I'm in the notion to make this here confession." He sniffed the bottle again. "Syrup. Dogged if you didn't outsmart me on that one."

CHAPTER 13

GONE

The sheriff was out when Grandmother called his office, and it was more than an hour later when he arrived at Fineweather. By the time he, Grandmother, and Rose drove out to the Peabody Place, only a wisp of smoke drifted from the chimney. Sheriff Tate pecked on the door, then swung it open and stepped inside.

"Mr. Birdsong!" Rose called. "Mr. Birdsong, we're back."

"Looks to me like he's gone," Grandmother said.

"He can't be," said Rose.

The sheriff poked the coals in the fireplace with a stick. "Been gone quite a while, I'd say."

"He promised to confess."

"Confess what?" Grandmother said. "If he was telling the truth, he needn't have run off like this."

"But he's so sick," Rose said.

The sheriff picked up the bottle of syrup, which lay near the smoldering coals. "Aside from a few bad habits, I'll wager Dooley Birdsong, as he called himself, is as healthy as you and me."

"Why do you say that, Hollis?" Grandmother started to sit on the couch and then thought better of it.

"May as well tell you, I reckon. I had hoped there would be no need."

"Tell us what?"

"When you called a while ago, I was over at Nate Everett's store. He had been concerned for some time that Birdsong wasn't paying for the goods he bought—just offering excuses and promises. Nate put off calling me as long as he could. When he quit letting Birdsong buy on credit, he got angry, made some threats."

"Poor old Nate," Grandmother said. "He never hurt anybody."

"I told you, Grandmother," Rose said. "Birdsong's crazy!"

"I decided to do a little investigating," the sheriff continued. "Didn't take long to trace our man back to a couple of little towns in Missouri. Small towns always have a few trusting souls like old Mr. Everett, and apparently Birdsong knows it. He went by the name Dudley Blanchard. When the townspeople tried to force him to pay up, Blanchard—Birdsong—no one seems to know what his real name is—disappeared."

"Well, I'll say!"

"Oh, wait. It gets better. I also found a record in Tennessee of a fellow by the name of Darcy Breedlove. What'll you bet me it's the same guy?"

"How did he manage to buy land here?"

"Good question. Apparently, he's a real smooth talker when he needs to be. He never made a payment, from what I understand. Always had a sob story."

"But—but I trusted him!" Rose cried.

The sheriff shook his head. "Some people are just too ornery to get along with anybody. I see it all the time."

"Do you think you can catch him, Hollis? He can't get far on foot."

"Of course we'll try, but apparently he isn't on foot. Nate said he thought he saw him driving some kind of car. According to Missouri records, Blanchard owned one that he'd stopped paying for a long time ago. He could have had it hidden anywhere in these woods. And we have no idea which direction he went."

"But I *trusted* him," Rose repeated angrily.

Grandmother put her arm around Rose's shoulders. "I know, dear. I guess it was just no use."

Rose went outside and sat on the porch, where a hot breeze blew up from the woods. As Grandmother and Sheriff Tate stepped out of the shack, the sheriff was saying that he needed to get back to town.

"I'm ready to go, too," said Grandmother.

"Can I stay a while longer?" Rose asked. "It will be good to have this place back again."

Grandmother looked at the Sheriff.

"Given Birdsong's record," the Sheriff said, "I don't think we need to worry about him coming back."

"You didn't want him to stay long," Grandmother said to Rose. "Looks like you got your wish."

It was a short distance through the woods to the dirt road where the sheriff's car was parked. After the sound of the motor faded away, Rose walked down to the creek, where Ring sat with her feet dangling in the water, as usual.

"That old geezer sure pulled a fast one on you," Ring said as Rose dropped down nearby.

"He didn't care who thought I burned his house. All he cared about was himself."

"At least you're in the clear now."

"But I'm still moving to Jonesboro."

"Surely what's waiting for you there can't be as bad as what you've been through here."

"It sure didn't make me love my fellow man."

"But all people are not like that, Rose. Everyone deserves a chance."

"I'll never be able to do it. School starts soon. Then what do I do? Run like a scared rabbit?"

"You don't give yourself much credit, do you?"

"What do you mean?"

"Okay, so this thing with Mr. B. didn't turn out quite the way it should have. But you faced it on your own. And you didn't 'run like a scared rabbit' then. I think you handled yourself quite well."

"You do?" Ring nodded. "All the same, maybe you could work some more voodoo to change my future."

"It wasn't voodoo. Anyway, I don't think you need that anymore."

Rose heaved a sigh and plopped a pebble between her knees into the water. "I'm sure going to miss you when summer's over."

"That's not for a while yet."

"It's all passing too quickly. I came here in June fully intending to spend a long, miserable summer. It hasn't been that way at all, thanks to you. And my grandmother has been great."

"It *has* been a good summer. Much like others I remember, yet different in many ways."

"Where will you go when I leave?" Rose asked.

"I'm not going anywhere." Ring stood up quickly and looked toward the setting sun. "It's getting late."

"See you tomorrow?" asked Rose.

"See you tomorrow," Ring replied.

CHAPTER 14

THE PARTING

But the tomorrows ran out all too soon for Rose. She spent day after day, hour after hour with Ring; but no matter how much she wanted to, she was not able to stop her summer at Fineweather from coming to an end.

Saturday, August 21, 1971

"It's the twenty-first of August," Ring said one hot, still day at the creek. "Tomorrow is your last day."

"Don't remind me," Rose said.

"Unfortunately, it would happen even if I didn't."

"I know. Life goes on, and the earth keeps turning." As if the earth needed her help, Rose stood up and spread her hands toward the sky, turning a wide, sweeping circle and shouting toward the treetops, "Whether Rose Carlisle lives or dies, the world will keep on turning."

Ring gazed through the woods toward the Peabody Place. "And other girls like you will come and go."

"You mean other girls like *us*, don't you?"

Ring's gaze met Rose's now, and a sad smile found its way to her lips. "Yeah. Like *us*."

"You know, thanks to you, I've learned a lot this summer."

Ring sat quietly waiting to hearing what Rose would say next.

Rose sat on a big rock and plopped her bare feet into the cool water. "I've learned that I can't always control what happens, but I can control what I do about it. I have only one life, and whatever happens—good or bad—it's up to me to make the best of it."

Ring smiled. "A very valuable lesson."

"Trouble is, it won't be so easy without you to tell me what to do."

"I haven't told you what to do. Everything you did this summer, you did on your own."

"What about the spell you cast on me that day at the Peabody Place?"

"I keep telling you, I did *not* cast a spell on you. I only pulled that stunt because you thought you needed it. Your own imagination made it seem real."

"You and I have been so close all these weeks. It's funny—it's almost as if you are part of me. A part I never knew was there. Like a long-lost twin sister or something. Does that make sense?"

"Believe it or not, it makes a lot of sense to me."

"I don't want to leave you, Ring." Rose buried her face in her hands as her tears began to fall. "Please, think of a way so I don't have to leave you." She leaned over so that her arms and head rested on her knees. Tears trickled down her cheeks and disappeared into the creek at her feet.

Suddenly aware of a dreadful silence about her, she jerked her head up and looked around. "Ring?" she called. She jumped off the rock where she had been sitting and ran up the pathway a short distance.

"Ring, where are you?" She was screaming now. "Ring!" Her heart beat so fast that it felt as if it would jump out of her chest. "Oh, no! I didn't mean this way!" She threw on her sneakers and ran for the Peabody Place. "Come back, Ring. Not like this! Please! Come back!" After searching through the shack, she realized that Ring was gone for good.

Going back outside, she walked around the shack and stopped beside the big oak tree. Kneeling beside the mound of dry earth that was Petal's grave, she let the last of her tears drop onto the hot, dusty ground. She walked a little way into the woods and found a small bush that had a lot of green branches. She broke off a flexible twig and tied it around the middle of two sticks to form a small cross. Then she went back and stuck the cross into the ground near Petal's grave. She mounded some stones around the base of the cross.

"Good-bye, Petal," she said softly, giving in to another flood of tears. She knew that eventually the cross of sticks would fall apart and the grave would be covered with leaves and weeds, leaving no evidence that Petal was buried there. As she stood up, she removed her glasses and wiped her eyes with a dirty hand. Replacing her glasses and pushing them up firmly, she began to walk away.

Part way up the path, she realized that she was leaving the shack wide open. She went inside and tugged all the windows down. When she went back outside, she closed the door soundly, and walked briskly away without another backward glance.

CHAPTER 15

THE RIDDLE

"Rose?" Grandmother's voice called later that evening from the hallway outside the room that had been Rose's all summer.

"Come in, Grandmother," Rose answered. As her grandmother swished in and sat down on the side of the big bed, Rose said, "Grandmother, did I ever tell you how much I love your perfume?"

"Why, no, I don't believe you have. Do you think your mother would let you wear it if I gave it to you?"

"I think so. And every time I wear it, I'll think of you."

"You're not going away forever, you know. You may come back next summer or during the holidays. Any time you want to."

"I'll look forward to it."

"Since you will be leaving tomorrow, I thought we might talk a while. That is, if you haven't anything else to do." Her eyes scanned the room. "Packing maybe?"

"I'm finished." Rose climbed onto the bed and leaned back against the pillows.

"It certainly has been a short summer," Grandmother said.

"Yes, it has. But wonderful. I wasn't sure at first, but I got over that."

"I noticed." Grandmother fluffed a ruffled blue pillow and put it behind Rose's shoulders. "I've hardly even seen you the past few weeks."

"I hope you didn't mind."

"No, no, not at all. I wanted you to do whatever made you happy."

"I *have* been happy until . . ."

"Until?"

"Until Ring left. Even when I lost Petal, I still had Ring—until today."

"I know. It's very hard to give up someone you care about."

"I didn't think anything could ever hurt as bad as when Dad walked out on us."

"And now Ring?"

"But it's sort of funny, Grandmother. I know I'll probably never see her again, but somehow it's like Ring is still with me. We were close for so long. I never knew anyone like her."

Grandmother nodded. "Wise beyond her years."

"You sound as if you knew her."

"I think I did. Or at least someone like her—many years ago."

"Huh?"

"Rose, what I'm about to tell you may sound a bit incredible, but I want you to know before you leave tomorrow."

Rose sat up and crossed her legs, resting her elbows on her knees and her chin in her hands.

"Where is the doll you found in that old trunk at the Peabody Place? Are you taking her with you?"

Rose opened the drawer near the bed and pulled the doll out. "No, she belongs here."

"As you wish." Grandmother reached into the pocket of her blue housecoat and brought out the scrap of fabric that she had found in the trunk in her own attic. "These pieces of material are the same. They don't look it now. The sunlight has faded the doll's dress. This piece—" she held up the scrap "—has been in that old trunk upstairs no telling how long."

"What does it have to do with Ring?"

"Hold on a second. Let me start at the beginning. Many years ago, when I lived here as a child, I was much like you. In fact, since I've come to know you this summer, I'm convinced that you are more like me than your mother ever was."

"I like being like you."

Grandmother smiled and brushed Rose's hair from her cheek. Her hand smelled of rose-scented lotion. "I was mostly happy here then, as everyone has been."

"That's why they named it Fineweather."

"Um-hm. But one summer—I was just about your age—was unusually difficult for me. It was a time of new emotions and mixed feelings about everything. I wasn't moving to a new home, but I had some problems which I felt no one could understand."

"That sure sounds familiar."

"Yes, I suppose in that respect young girls will always be the same. No matter what else may change—like Fineweather has over the years—people are pretty much the same.

"You still haven't told me where Ring fits into all this?"

"We'll, since I felt no one could help me, I spent a lot of time off by myself."

"At the Peabody Place?"

Grandmother shook her head. "Someone was living there at the time. I stayed down at the creek a lot and over in the meadow near where Mr. Birdsong lived this summer."

"Were you lonely?"

"Lonelier than anyone could imagine—except you."

"Then what happened?"

"Then I met someone."

"Grandpa?"

Grandmother laughed. "Oh, no. We knew each other all our lives, but we didn't start dating for a few more years. This was a girl. A girl very much like me. She seemed to know me, although we had never met before."

"That sounds like Ring. What was your friend's name?"

"Her name was Ring."

"What a coincidence. Do you suppose she was the grandmother of *my* Ring?"

Grandmother shrugged. "That's the strange part." She pulled something from her pocket. "Do you remember the day we found this?"

"It's a picture of some girl. It fell from the album that rainy day we were in the attic."

"There was a similar one mounted in the album. I didn't know these pictures existed before, but I've done considerable studying about them since then."

"Have you figured out who the girls are?"

"Well, according to the old papers, the trunk in the attic belonged to my grandmother. She was the one in the big hat."

"Her brother Tom was posing with her."

"Um-hm. I think the girl in the album is also my grandmother, years earlier." Grandmother gazed at the picture she held in her hand. "This girl looks enough like her to be a sister, though her only sister was much older."

"Who else could it be?"

"I think it's someone my grandmother told me about once. If she told me the girl's name, I've forgotten it. I'm certain it didn't mean much to me at the time. Yet, years later, bits and pieces of her story came back to me that summer. Sadly, it was too late to ask her about it then. And now your experience seems strangely similar."

"But I don't understand."

"Nor do I. Logically it makes no sense at all. It almost seems as if this girl has appeared time and again to members of our family."

"That isn't Ring in the picture."

"Not the way you or I knew her. But my grandmother would have seen her differently."

"So you think Ring has been passed down, sort of like this doll?" Rose hugged the doll.

"So it appears. I wish I knew whether her existence is a part of this place or something that our minds conjure up in our time of need."

"Why didn't you tell me all this before?"

"At first, I was waiting to see if you had indeed met Ring. Then I felt it best to let things develop naturally."

"Mr. Birdsong saw Ring."

"Are you sure?"

"No, I guess not. How could there be a picture of her?"

"That's another part of the puzzle."

"And she was here at the house. I could never get her to come back with me."

Grandmother stared at the picture of the auburn-haired girl in the white dress. "Of course, I have no proof that this is the girl my grandmother told me about. There was lots of family here then, as well as some employees. I'm certain no one saw *my* summer friend except me."

"Did you tell your mother about her?"

"My mother would have insisted that I had had too much sun, as will yours if you choose to tell her."

"Why didn't they know Ring?"

"My mother didn't live here until she was grown and married, and yours only lived here as an infant.

"It does all sound a little, like you said, incredible. But you and I know it's so."

"Indeed we do. I'm thankful to have someone to share it with at last."

"Did you ever see Ring again?"

"I never did."

"I won't forget her, Grandmother."

"Nor will I." Grandmother reached over and hugged her granddaughter. "I feel very fortunate—very special—for having known her."

"So do I. She was the best friend any girl ever had."

ABOUT THE AUTHOR

 A retired school counselor and Licensed Professional Counselor, Sam Sullivan lives on a farm in northeast Arkansas with his wife of 47 years, Jan. They have two grown sons and one grandson.

Sullivan is one of the song leaders at the local church. Besides writing, he enjoys playing the piano, driving his tractor, and loafing.

www.ingramcontent.com/pod-product-compliance
Lightning Source LLC
Chambersburg PA
CBHW020620120726
47905CB00003B/874